W9-BPN-625

THE CHRISTMAS CHRONICLES

Parts 1 and 2

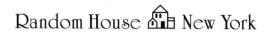

Adapted by David Lewman • Illustrated by Grace Mills, Fabio Laguna, and Alan Batson

"The Christmas Chronicles" screenplay by Matt Lieberman • Directed by Clay Kaytis

"The Christmas Chronicles: Part 2" written by Matt Lieberman and Chris Columbus • Directed by Chris Columbus

Random House 🏠 New York

THE CHRISTMAS CHRONICLES: TM/© Netflix. Used with permission. Published in the United States by Random House Children's Books, a division of Penguin Random House LLC, 1745 Broadway, New York, NY 10019, and in Canada by Penguin Random House Canada Limited, Toronto. Random House and the colophon are registered trademarks of Penguin Random House LLC.
The Christmas Chronicles, Netflix, and all related titles, logos, and characters are trademarks of Netflix, Inc.
rhcbooks.com
ISBN 978-0-593-30988-9 (trade) — ISBN 978-0-593-43450-5 (ebook)

Book design by Catherine Mucciardi

Printed in the United States of America
10 9 8 7 6 5 4 3 2 1

Random House Children's Books supports the First Amendment and celebrates the right to read.

2021 Edition

One Christmas Eve . . .

Kate was watching old videotapes. She liked remembering past Christmases, back when her whole family was together and her older brother, Teddy, still believed in Santa Claus.

Kate believed, with all her heart. She wished Teddy did, too.

Suddenly, a flash of red on the tape caught Kate's eye! Was that a gloved hand? Putting a present under the tree? Could it be . . . SANTA?

"Teddy!" Kate yelled to her brother upstairs. **"YOU GOTTA SEE THIS!"**

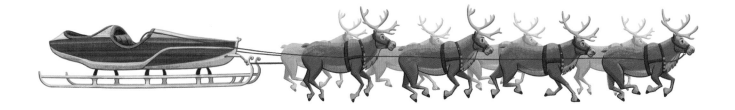

Kate convinced Teddy that they should catch Santa on tape this year. They set up their old video camera to record the Christmas tree all night. Then they ran fishing line across the room and tied it to a jingle bell. In the middle of the night, the bell woke Kate. *RING-A-LING!*

SANTA!

Kate and Teddy could hear him on the roof. They ran out into the cold night and saw his sleigh hovering over the alley. Santa was zipping from chimney to chimney, moving so fast, he looked like a red blur.

To get a closer look, Kate climbed a telephone pole and jumped into the sleigh.

"What are you doing?" Teddy cried. He scrambled onto a garage roof and leaped—and found himself dangling from one of the sleigh's runners. Kate pulled him up and they ducked behind the seat.

Soon Santa jumped in and tossed his huge red bag of toys in the back without noticing Kate and Teddy. He clucked to his reindeer, flicked the reins, and zoomed into the night sky!

Kate was freezing. She crawled forward and tapped Santa on the shoulder to ask for a blanket. Startled, Santa cried out and yanked on the reins. The reindeer flew straight up!

WHOOSH! A jet plane roared by, almost hitting them. Santa's hat blew off. His bag of toys tumbled out of the sleigh. The reins snapped, and the reindeer flew away!

Then . . . *WHAM!* The sleigh crashed to the ground, skidding into a snowbank.

Kate and Teddy were amazed to find themselves face to face with Santa Claus. He had long white hair, a thick beard, and a big red suit. Just like they'd pictured him.

"Boy," he sighed. "You two really messed things up. Now I've got to get my hat back, find my bag of presents, and round up the reindeer. Or else Christmas will be ruined!" Santa started to walk off.

Kate jumped to her feet. "Let us help you!"

Santa turned back and shrugged. "Suit yourself."

They came upon a crook who bragged about how he'd stolen a sports car. Teddy managed to snatch the keys while the guy wasn't looking, and they sped off. Teddy drove.

"Isn't this stealing?" Santa protested.

"This car's already stolen," Teddy said. "We're just borrowing it until we find your reindeer."

Kate was the first to spot them. "There they are!"

Just then, a police car rounded a corner. Santa told Kate to go after the reindeer. "Teddy and I will buy you some time."

Santa drove, peeling away from the police. On their computer, the officers learned that the red car had been reported as stolen. They tore off after it. *VRROOOOM!*

Kate gave Comet a candy cane, and she let Kate climb onto her back. Holding Comet's antlers, Kate rode off, leading all the reindeer back to Santa. She couldn't believe she was actually riding COMET!

Santa was enjoying his fast drive through the streets. But he suddenly had to swerve to avoid another car. *WHOMP!* He slammed into a pile of snow and the car's engine conked out.

WHOOOOT! With its siren blaring, the police car pulled up. . . .

Just as the police were about to arrest Santa and Teddy, Kate galloped up on Comet.

Santa slipped a glowing ornament into Teddy's hand. "Take this," he whispered. "Find my bag. It'll lead you to the elves."

Teddy took the ornament and jumped onto Donner's back!

Racing off, Kate and Teddy saw more police ahead. They had to get the reindeer to fly!

"Attach Comet's jingle bells!" Santa shouted.

Kate saw Comet's bells dangling. When she snapped the buckle together, the bells glowed green. "C'mon, Comet! Fly!" she urged. The reindeer rose into the air, carrying Kate and Teddy right over the police cars!

But the police arrested Santa and drove him to the station.

PING! The ornament chimed. They were getting closer to Santa's bag! They decided to land and find it on foot.

Santa made the best of his time in jail, spreading cheer by singing a rocking Christmas song.

The ornament led Kate and Teddy to a park, where Kate spotted Santa's bag stuck in a tree. Teddy climbed up and pushed the bag to the ground.

Kate peered into the bag. "Hello?" she called. "Elves?" No answer. She crawled in. Then, with a chiming sound and a flash of green light . . . Kate disappeared!

"KATE!" Teddy cried.

Kate crawled through a tunnel of presents. She spotted an elf, but it ran away. "Hey! Come back!" she called.

She pushed through a wall of presents and fell into a swirling vortex of Christmas gifts rising from a bright light far below! Kate swam through the air, working her way down, until she reached . . .

. . . Santa's toy room at the North Pole! She gasped.

Thousands of presents were riding up a spiral conveyor belt until they rose through the vortex and landed on Santa's bag.

"So cool," Kate murmured.

She heard whispering behind her. She turned and saw hundreds of elves! Maybe even thousands! Thinking Kate was an intruder, they tied her up with a string of Christmas lights!

Kate explained to the elves that Santa had sent her, and that he needed their help. To see if Kate was telling the truth, they looked her up in Santa's big book of True Believers. There was her name! They also saw the names of her whole family—except Teddy's.

When they saw that Kate was a True Believer, the elves cheered! Time to HELP SANTA!

VVRRRRANG! A chain saw cut into Santa's jail cell, and an elf dropped Santa's hat through the hole.

"Merry Christmas, everyone," Santa said to the other inmates, pulling on his hat. "Try to be good!" He touched a finger to his nose, and . . . *WHOOSH!* Santa was swept up and out in a sparkling red blur!

Outside, Kate and Teddy showed Santa his sleigh, fixed good as new by the elves. The toys were loaded and the reindeer were hitched up. But when Santa checked his watch, he said he'd never be able to deliver all the presents by sunrise.

"What if we helped you?" Teddy asked.

"You mean, you believe in me?" Santa asked.

Teddy nodded. "Totally."

Santa smiled. "Then let's DO THIS!"

With Teddy driving and Kate tossing out presents, Santa was able to deliver everything before the sun rose on Christmas morning!

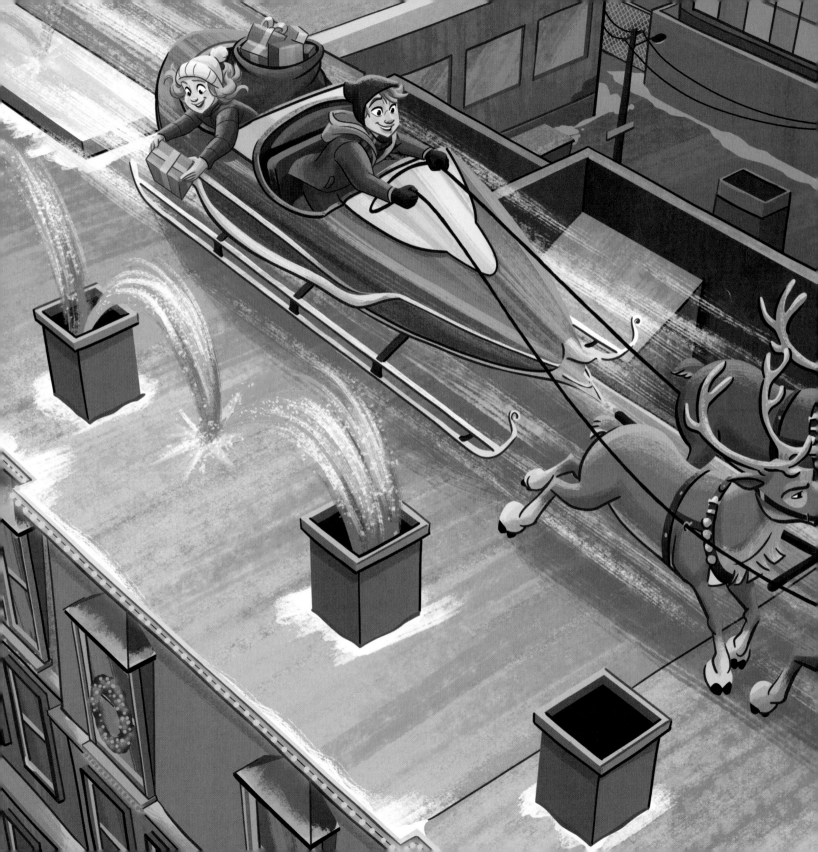

Back home, Kate said, "That was the best night of my whole life."

"Mine too," Teddy agreed.

"Christmas Eve is always the best night of my life," Santa said. He flicked the reins of his sleigh and flew off. Then he circled back and shouted, "HO! HO! HO! MERRY CHRISTMAS!"

And then he was gone, headed home to the North Pole.

Kate sighed. "Best Christmas ever!" She checked her video camera. "Hey!" she said. "He took the tape!"

Once Santa was home, he placed the videotape on his desk, smiling. Then he took out a feather pen, dipped it into an inkwell, and wrote Teddy's name in his big book of True Believers.

Two years later . . .

Near the South Pole, an elf named Speck trudged through the deep snow and freezing wind to reach a cave. Inside, a teenage boy named Belsnickel was looking at old photos of himself—back when he was one of Santa's elves. A tear rolled down his cheek.

"Belsnickel?" Speck said, tugging at the boy's pant leg.

"AHH!" Belsnickel yelled. Then he frowned. "Speck, don't sneak up on me like that. What took you so long? Did you get it?"

The little elf unwrapped a videotape labeled "12/24/18" and handed it to Belsnickel, who popped it into an old VCR. Multiple television screens showed Kate, tied up with Christmas lights, saying, "I'm in the book! I'm a TRUE BELIEVER!"

Belsnickel's face broke into an evil grin. "She's perfect!"

"Lamest Christmas ever," Kate grumbled. She was at a sunny resort in Mexico, missing snow and ice-skating and her friends. Her mom was spending all her time with her new friend, Bob. Kate was stuck with Bob's ten-year-old son, Jack, who was scared of everything.

That evening, Kate saw a star, closed her eyes, and wished for Santa to get her out of there. "Or I'm gonna run away!"

Belsnickel, spying on Kate, arranged for Bob to win a tour of the Mayan ruins for himself and Kate's mother, Claire; a snorkeling adventure for Teddy and his girlfriend; and a Kids' Club slumber party for Kate and Jack.

Stuck with Jack again? That did it. Kate decided to fly home. The driver of a nearby golf cart said he was filling in for the usual airport shuttle. Kate got in.

The driver was . . . BELSNICKEL!

Claiming he knew a shortcut, Belsnickel drove into the jungle.

"Are you sure this is the way to the airport?" Kate asked.

"AIRPORT?" Jack said, popping up from the back seat. He had followed her! "Kate, are you running away?"

Before she could answer, Belsnickel threw a lump of coal in front of the golf cart, and *BOOM!* A green wormhole opened! Belsnickel swerved the cart, causing Kate and Jack to tumble into the wormhole!

"AHHHH!" they screamed.

When they fell out of the other end of the wormhole, they discovered they were at the North Pole! It was freezing.

"HELP!" Kate cried. "SOMEBODY SAVE US!"

Santa, out hunting Jola the terrible Yule Cat, heard Kate. He found her and Jack, now both passed out from the cold. While Santa was putting them into his sleigh, Belsnickel stowed away on the bottom rudder!

Santa zoomed home, passing through the shimmering aurora borealis that shielded his village. Belsnickel dropped off the sleigh before Santa landed. He and Speck met up with Jola the fierce Yule Cat.

"My plan is going perfectly!" Belsnickel gloated.

Mrs. Claus revived Kate and Jack with her special cocoa. Then she and Santa gave them a tour, pointing out the cannons that shot snow and, at the top of a huge tree, the Christmas Star, which powered everything.

After an amazing dinner, Mrs. Claus tucked Kate and Jack in and told them bedtime stories. One was about how Santa had long ago received the Christmas Star from the Forest Elves in Turkey. Another was about how Belsnickel had broken the Elves' Code and turned into a human.

And at that very moment, Belsnickel was carrying out his evil plan. . . .

The former elf sent Speck to shoot Elf's Bane out of the rooftop cannons. He told Jola the monstrous cat to attack the reindeer. And Belsnickel himself stole the Christmas Star! He planned to take it to the South Pole and make his own village.

The Elf's Bane made the elves wild. Jola fought Dasher, injuring her. And when Santa tried to take the Christmas Star back from Belsnickel, it ended up exploding into a million pieces! The village went dark, losing its aurora borealis shield.

Belsnickel zipped away on a drone.

Mrs. Claus said she'd tend to Dasher and find a cure for the Elf's Bane problem with Jack's help. Santa and Kate flew to Turkey with seven reindeer to get another Christmas Star from the Forest Elves.

But they didn't know they had a stowaway.

Mrs. Claus muttered a healing chant over Dasher. She gave Jack a map, telling him to go and pick Levande Root, an arctic flower that was the only antidote for Elf's Bane. Jack was scared, but Mrs. Claus gave him three Christmas cookies: a glowing Christmas tree, an explosive gingerbread man, and a snowman that would give him courage.

Distracting the wild elves with other cookies, she sent the frightened boy on his way, telling him, "I believe in you, Jack. Be my hero."

As he headed out into the dark night, Jack told himself, "It's hero time!"

In Turkey, Santa and Kate met with Hakan, the ancient leader of the Forest Elves. Hakan agreed to build Santa a new Christmas Star.

"But we must move quickly!" Santa urged.

Even with a map, Jack worried about getting lost. He used the glowing Christmas tree cookie to leave a trail of crumbs.

He reached a towering glacier. Over a hundred feet up, a red flower shone in the moonlight. The Levande Root! Jack gulped. "That is really high up," he said to himself. He remembered the snowman cookie. After swallowing a bite, he felt brave! "Let's do this!"

He started to climb.

Near the plant, Jack looked up and saw Jola the giant Yule Cat! "Nice kitty . . . ," he said, plucking the plant and sliding down the glacier.

Jola chased him! *ROWWRR!*

When Jack reached the bottom, he threw the exploding gingerbread man cookie at the monstrous cat. *BOOM!* Jola ran away.

Jack rushed back to the village and gave the Levande Root to Mrs. Claus.

Hakan's Forest Elves made Santa a new Christmas Star. But as he and Kate flew away . . . *WHAM!* Belsnickel rammed into them with his own sleigh! He slapped a Time Twister onto Santa's sleigh and flew off with the star!

The Time Twister took Kate and Santa back to . . .

. . . 1990, where Kate met her father as a boy her own age! He gave her hope to continue her adventure. She got new batteries for the Time Twister, and Santa set it for fifteen seconds after Belsnickel had stolen the Christmas Star.

WHOOSH! Santa and Kate zoomed through a wormhole, arriving just in time to pluck the Christmas Star out of Belsnickel's hands. Then they raced back to the North Pole with Belsnickel close behind!

Kate parachuted out of the sleigh and rushed to the tree to attach the new Christmas Star while Santa kept Belsnickel busy.

At the same time, Jack made his way past the frendzied elves to load the rooftop cannons with Mrs. Claus's antidote.

When Belsnickel realized what Kate was doing, he tried to stop her with one of his drones, but Jack shot it out of the sky with the soft-missile bow Mrs. Claus had given him.

BOOM! The cannons released the antidote. It snowed down onto the elves, and they returned to their regular selves, forgetting all the mischief they'd caused while affected by the Elf's Bane.

ZWOOOOM! Kate attached the new Christmas Star to the tree, and power was restored to the village. The lights came back on, and the aurora borealis once again shimmered in the sky, protecting Santa's hidden town.

Belsnickel was sure he was in big trouble. But Santa handed him a Christmas gift—a wonderful butterfly.

"The first toy we built together," Belsnickel said, surprised. "You kept it."

Santa nodded. "It reminds me of what an amazing elf you are."

"We love you, Belsnickel," Mrs. Claus said. Santa agreed, and so did all the elves.

"I've always loved you guys," Belsnickel said, realizing it for the first time. He apologized to Dasher for Jola's attack. A jingle bell rang, and . . .

. . . Belsnickel turned back into an elf!

Kate was so happy to see the family of elves reunited. She realized she'd been wrong to run away from her own family.

She remembered something her father had once said:

"Christmas isn't about where you are, but who you're with."

It was time to go home.

Mrs. Claus gave Jack and Kate cookies for the sleigh ride back to Mexico. Jack asked what kind of magic they had.

"None," Mrs. Claus said, smiling. "Just like the snowman cookie."

"What!" Jack cried. "I thought that cookie gave me courage!"

Mrs. Claus shook her head. "The hero was always inside you."

Back in Mexico, Kate was thrilled to see her mom and Bob. On the beach that night, under a full moon, Kate, Teddy, Claire, Bob, and Jack sang Christmas carols together.

And up at the North Pole, Santa, Mrs. Claus, Belsnickel, and the rest of the elves did the very same thing.

The End